Bad News Nails

Also by Jill Santopolo

Sparkle Spa

✳ ⋅ ✳ ⋅ ✳ ⋅ ✳ ⋅ ✳ ⋅ ✳

Book 5

Bad News Nails

JILL SANTOPOLO

Aladdin
NEW YORK   LONDON   TORONTO   SYDNEY   NEW DELHI

ALADDIN

An imprint of Simon & Schuster Children's Publishing Division

1230 Avenue of the Americas, New York, NY 10020

This Aladdin hardcover edition February 2015

Text copyright © 2015 by Simon & Schuster, Inc.

Jacket illustrations copyright © 2015 by Cathi Mingus

All rights reserved, including the right of reproduction in whole or in part in any form.

ALADDIN is a trademark of Simon & Schuster, Inc., and related logo is a registered trademark of Simon & Schuster, Inc.

Also available in an Aladdin paperback edition.

For information about special discounts for bulk purchases, please contact Simon & Schuster Special Sales at 1-866-506-1949 or business@simonandschuster.com.

The Simon & Schuster Speakers Bureau can bring authors to your live event. For more information or to book an event, contact the Simon & Schuster Speakers Bureau at 1-866-248-3049 or visit our website at www.simonspeakers.com.

Series designed by Jeanine Henderson

Jacket designed by Laura Lyn DiSiena

The text of this book was set in Adobe Caslon.

Manufactured in the United States of America 0115 FFG

10 9 8 7 6 5 4 3 2 1

Library of Congress Control Number 2014956305

ISBN 978-1-4814-2385-4 (hc)

ISBN 978-1-4814-2384-7 (pbk)

ISBN 978-1-4814-2386-1 (eBook)

This one's for you, editrix Karen.

Special sparkly thanks to Miriam Altshuler,
Marianna Baer, Amy Ewing, Anne Heltzel,
Marie Rutkoski, and Eliot Schrefer.

Contents

Bad News Nails

one

Sprinkle Sprinkle Little Star

"Can you believe we get to go to a fiesta?" Aly Tanner's younger sister, Brooke, asked as they stood in the Sparkle Spa staring at the nail polish display.

"It's a gala," Aly told her, laughing. "Not a fiesta."

Brooke laughed too. "Oh, right. A gala. Don't you think 'fiesta' sounds more fun though?"

Aly kind of thought it did. But it didn't sound as fancy as a gala—the Businesswomen Unite Fund-Raising Gala, to be exact. "It does," Aly said. "But

I don't think people get to wear fancy dresses to a fiesta."

Because Brooke and Aly had started their own business, the Sparkle Spa, in the back room of their mother's nail salon, True Colors, Mom said the girls could come with her to the gala. She'd even let them buy new, sparkly dresses to wear. Joan, the girls' favorite manicurist, who also helped Mom run True Colors, was coming too.

"Do you think we should start polishing?" Brooke asked.

Even though the Sparkle Spa was usually open on Friday afternoons, the girls had closed it today so that they could get ready for the gala. They were going to get dressed at the Sparkle Spa and do each other's hair and nails.

"Toes first?" Aly asked.

Brooke nodded. "I just need to pick out my colors."

2

Aly pulled their dresses out of the closet. Brooke's was yellow and ruffly, with gold glitter all over the skirt. She had shiny gold sandals to wear too. Aly's dress was orange, which wasn't usually her favorite color, but she especially loved this dress. It was silky and came down to her ankles and had a gold glittery belt. Her sandals were the same as Brooke's, but in a larger size, since she was a fifth grader and her sister was a third grader.

"How about Lemon Aid?" Aly asked, pulling the bottle of polish from the shelf and holding it up to Brooke's dress.

Brooke shook her head. "Too much yellow."

Brooke was a very good "color picker." She helped a lot of the customers at the Sparkle Spa choose their nail polish and sometimes even helped the customers in True Colors. And she was usually the one to decide on the Sparkle Spa's Color of the Week. This week it was a multicolored glittery shade called Sprinkle Sprinkle Little Star.

"I think pink looks nice with yellow," Brooke said, picking up Under Watermelon. "Maybe this color on my toes. And the Color of the Week for my fingernails! I think I'm set now. How about you?"

Aly looked at her dress. "What color do you think goes best with orange?" she asked.

Brooke picked up Please Don't Teal. "This one," she said. "And you should use Sprinkle Sprinkle Little Star for your nails too. We can match!"

Aly smiled. "Okay," she said. "Take off your flip-flops. You can go first."

Brooke climbed into the blue-green pedicure chair that was almost the same color as Please Don't Teal. Aly turned the water on to fill up the basin.

"Let's make a list," she said, "of everything we're excited for tonight."

Aly loved making lists. They helped her organize her thoughts. Brooke's brain seemed like it was hardly ever organized, but she was actually pretty good at helping Aly make lists.

"One," Brooke said, swinging her legs back and forth, "we get to wear the fanciest dresses we've ever had."

"Two," Aly added as she squirted soap into the water, "we get to be counted as official businesswomen who started their own company."

Brooke looked at Aly. "Do you think we should bring our business cards?"

"Good idea," Aly said. "I think we have some in the desk."

A little more than a month ago, Brooke had broken her arm. Because of that, Aly had needed help from some of their friends to run the Sparkle Spa, which led to the girls deciding to create official job titles and business cards for themselves and their friends who had helped.

She and Brooke were now co–chief executive officers. As CEOs, they were in charge of pretty much everything in the spa: the Color of the Week, special occasion manicures, the jewelry-making station, and customer service. Most important was the fundraising jar, which held the money their customers donated for manicures and pedicures. When the jar filled up, Aly and Brooke would pick a worthy charity or cause and donate the money there.

"It's a good thing Mom bought us little purses to match our shoes," Brooke said. "We can keep the cards in there."

Mom really did think of everything. Aly wanted to be just like her when she grew up—smart and organized and successful.

"Three," Aly said, "I'm excited for the auction!"

As part of the gala, the attendees could "sell" things to help raise money for Businesswomen Unite, and Mom had offered to auction an internship at True Colors to anyone interested in learning how to run a small business. Aly thought that was really nice of her mom, teaching someone else how to be a business owner. She felt pretty lucky that Mom had taught her and Brooke for free.

"I hope the True Colors intern is as cool as Joan," Brooke said.

Aly had filed Brooke's toenails and now was painting them with a layer of clear polish so Under Watermelon would stick better.

"Me too," Aly said. "But that'll be hard. Joan's the coolest grown-up we know."

Just as Aly painted Brooke's big toe pink, Jenica Posner poked her head into the spa. Jenica was a sixth grader at their school, captain of the Auden

Elementary girls' soccer team, and the Sparkle Spa's first—and best—customer.

"Oh, good!" she said. "You're here! Charlotte said the Sparkle Spa was closed today, so I didn't know if you'd be around."

"Is your nana getting her nails done at True Colors?" Brooke asked from the pedicure chair.

Jenica nodded. "Anyway, I came to ask what you guys thought about having a spa party for the soccer team. We only have one more game this season—the state finals—and since it's such a big deal that we got that far, I thought we should celebrate."

"We could totally do that," Aly said. "What did you have in mind to make it different from your weekly pedicures?"

Jenica shrugged. "I don't know. But I'm sure you guys will think of something cool. You did invent the rainbow sparkle pedicure after all."

Brooke smiled—she was actually the one who had invented the pedicure, and for some reason, all the players on the team believed it had given them extra luck for their games this season. They'd been coming in every Tuesday afternoon to get their rainbow sparkle power refreshed ever since the salon opened. "We'll come up with something fantabulous," she told Jenica.

"When do you want to have the party?" Aly asked. Part of being in charge of their business meant organizing all of the practical things, like dates and times of special events.

"Well, the state finals are a week from tomorrow," Jenica said, leaning against the door frame, "so how about the day after? Next Sunday?"

Aly got up and looked at the wall calendar Charlotte had made. She had been named COO—chief operating officer—of the Sparkle Spa to make everything run smoothly on the days they were open, but she had to check her plans with Aly and Brooke first. There was nothing scheduled on the calendar yet for next Sunday.

"You got it," Aly said. "What time?"

Jenica tightened her ponytail. "How about eleven to one? And we'll order some pizza too."

"Sounds great to me," Aly said. Then she took a sparkle pen and wrote in *Soccer Spa Party* from the ten o'clock to two o'clock slots so they would have time for setup and cleanup too.

"Hey." Jenica looked around. "How come you're closed today if you guys are here?"

"We're going to a fiesta tonight!" Brooke answered. "And we have to make ourselves fancy!"

"A gala," Aly told Jenica. "She means a gala. It's for women who run businesses."

"And we get to wear sparkly dresses and stay out past our regular bedtimes because that's what happens when you run a business," Brooke said, pushing her glasses up on her nose.

Jenica looked impressed. "That's really awesome," she said.

Aly smiled. If anyone had told her at the beginning of the school year that the coolest sixth grader at Auden Elementary would think she was doing something awesome right now, she never would have believed it. But because of the Sparkle Spa, tons of people at school she'd never talked to before came up to her all the time, telling her how great her business was and asking if they could come by. Everyone, that is, except for Suzy Davis. Aly shook her head to get Suzy Davis out of her brain.

"Thanks," Aly said to Jenica.

"Yeah, thanks," Brooke said. "Aly, are you going to finish my pedicure? My big toe is the only one polished, and he feels lonely."

Jenica and Aly laughed. "On my way," Aly said.

"See you on Tuesday for our rainbow sparkles," Jenica told the girls. "And have fun tonight."

She left the Sparkle Spa, and Aly got back to work on Brooke's toes.

"Do you think we *will* have fun tonight?" Brooke asked.

Aly thought about it. "With fancy dresses and sparkly nails and staying out late, I think it might be our best night ever."

Brooke smiled. "Me too!"

two

Grayce Under Pressure

A few hours later the girls were all ready. Their nails were polished, and they were both wearing their sparkly dresses and gold sandals. Aly had braided beads into Brooke's hair, and Brooke had made Aly a beaded ribbon that she'd worn as a headband.

"I think we look beautiful," Brooke told Aly.

Aly had to agree.

"Yes, you do," Mrs. Tanner said as she and Joan entered the Sparkle Spa. "Beautiful and sparkly." Mom looked like she was going to cry.

"And so do you and Joan," Brooke added.

Wow! Aly thought. Aly hardly recognized her mother. She was wearing a Midnight Blues dress, and her hair was sleek and smooth around her long, dangly earrings.

Joan's shiny dress was the color of Red Hot Pepper nail polish. They each had Grayce Under Pressure on their nails, a new color Mom had ordered that was dark gray with a little bit of a shimmer.

"Who's ready to go to a fancy-pants party?" Joan asked.

"Me!" Brooke raised her hand.

"Then let's go!" Mom said. "I heard the food is going to be delicious."

Everyone carefully piled into Mom's car. She drove to Francie's, the nicest—and biggest—restaurant in their town. It was so big that at least seven True Colors regulars had gotten married there, including

Miss Lulu, who had had twelve bridesmaids!

When they reached the restaurant, a man wearing a tuxedo greeted Mom's car. He opened the doors for them and helped them out onto a long red carpet that led to the entrance to the restaurant.

"I feel like a movie star!" Brooke whispered to Aly.

Aly did too, but she also felt a little bit nervous. She'd never been to a party like this before. Even though she was the big sister, she grabbed Brooke's hand. Aly always felt better when she and Brooke stuck together like a team.

The girls walked into the restaurant with Mom and Joan behind them. First, Aly saw a woman in a long silver dress playing the piano. Then, as she gazed around, she saw a sea of women dressed in greens and blues, pinks and purples. Actually, it looked like their rainbow sparkle pedicure. She and Brooke were definitely the youngest people at the gala. And the shortest.

"Mini hot dogs!" Brooke shouted. "Over there!" She pointed to a table that was close by and then tugged on Aly's arm. "Let's go!"

Aly looked back at their mom, and Mrs. Tanner nodded. Aly let her sister pull her to a table filled with different sorts of treats: hamburgers, grilled cheese, meatballs, carrots—all bite-size versions. Brooke's eyes lit up at the food.

Brooke and Aly found little plates and took one of everything to try. As they ate, a woman in a gown the color of Green with Envy polish came over to them.

"You must be the Tanner sisters," she said. "When your mother told us about your salon, we were all very impressed."

Aly swallowed her mini grilled cheese sandwich and smiled. "Thanks," she said.

"Is it true that you have a group of other girls working for you?" the woman asked.

"We work together," Brooke said. "We're a team. Aly, Charlotte, Sophie, Lily, and me . . . and sometimes Caleb. He's a boy, but he helps out if we need him."

"That's really marvelous," the woman said, then she handed Aly a business card. "I run a magazine company. Perhaps we could feature your team one day."

"Okay," Aly said, putting the card in her gold purse. She gave the woman one of her business cards in return.

A very tall woman wearing a dress the color of Thunder and Whitening was listening to the conversation. She took a few steps closer.

"Let me tell you about *my* daughter," she said to the woman in green. "She's at the top of her class. I'm sure she'll follow in my footsteps and start a successful business of her own."

"Oh," said the woman in green. "Is she running a company now too?"

The woman in white paused. "Not yet," she said. "But she has some wonderful ideas already, and she's only eleven."

"I see," the woman in green answered, looking over at Aly and Brooke. "Well, if she makes any of them a reality like these girls, I'd be happy to consider a feature. But for now, I have to go speak to the party planner about the auction."

The woman in white nodded. "Of course," she said, and walked away.

Brooke took a bite of her mini burger. "That lady with the daughter did not seem very happy," she mumbled.

"Maybe she didn't like that we have a business and her daughter doesn't yet," Aly said.

Brooke shrugged. "Her daughter can start one too. I mean, if we can, she can."

"You're totally right, Brooke," Aly said.

The girls were sipping cherry juice mixed with club soda when the woman in the green dress walked onto the stage and tapped the microphone. The crowd quieted, and Mom and Joan joined Aly and Brooke.

"Welcome to the third annual Businesswomen Unite gala," she announced. "I hope everyone's been having a good time so far. We have a long list of items to auction off tonight, so let's get started!"

"I hope someone bids on the True Colors internship," Brooke whispered.

Her mom whispered back, "Me too."

"I hope I win the day in the bakery kitchen," Joan added. "I've never used a professional oven to make my cookies before."

Joan made the best cookies that Aly and Brooke had ever tasted. Mostly she baked just for fun, but sometimes people hired her to make desserts for parties. Aly secretly thought Joan should start her own bakery, but she'd never told anyone that because she didn't want Joan to leave the salon.

"The first item up for auction is donated by *Business Leaders* magazine, one of my company's publications. We will feature your business in both our print version and on our website. Let's start the bidding at fifty dollars."

Throughout the room, women raised their hands. The woman in green kept calling out larger sums of money. When the auction price reached two hundred fifty dollars, the only hand still raised was by a woman wearing a Teeny Tangeriney–colored dress.

As the auction continued throughout the evening, people bid on lots of items, but Brooke's and Aly's favorites were:

- Pencils inscribed with the winner's business name
- A pearl necklace

- A suitcase on wheels and matching backpack
- Dinner for four at Francie's

Then, finally, the Sweet Treats Kitchen & Bakery item was up.

"Good luck, Joan!" Aly whispered.

Brooke crossed her fingers and her legs for luck.

The bidding started at twenty-five dollars. Joan wasn't the only person interested, and Aly was a little worried that Joan wouldn't win. When the bidding got to three hundred dollars, Aly held her breath and closed her eyes.

But then Aly heard, "Sold to Joan West from True Colors nail salon."

Aly, Brooke, and their mom cheered for Joan.

"And speaking of True Colors," the woman in green said, "we're auctioning an internship at the nail salon. Learn how to run a real *hands-on* business.

Let's start the bidding at seventy-five dollars."

The unhappy woman wearing the Thunder and Whitening dress raised her hand. She called out, "May I bid on this for an eleven-year-old?"

Mom looked at the woman and answered, "If your daughter is eleven, she can intern with my girls at their Sparkle Spa."

Wait a minute! Aly thought. She'd been excited when the intern was going to be at True Colors, but she wouldn't know what to do with an intern at the Sparkle Spa. There were more than enough people working there already.

"Don't worry," Joan whispered to Aly. "If you need us, we'll help you out."

Aly bit her lip. Even with Joan's offer, she wasn't sure about this plan.

"I think it'd be cool to teach someone about the Sparkle Spa," Brooke said.

Aly thought about it. Maybe it *would* be fun to show another girl what they'd learned. But still! Mom should have asked first.

"In that case," the woman said, "I bid seven hundred and fifty dollars!"

Aly gasped. That was a *lot* of money.

"Going once, going twice," the lady in green said. "Sold to Carolyn Washington of Custom Creations."

"I hope we really like that lady's daughter," Brooke muttered to Aly.

"Me too," Aly answered.

Now that she'd gotten over her initial worry, she was imagining having someone fun working with them. There was always room for one more, wasn't there?

three

It's Not Easy Being Green

The next morning Aly was awakened by a soft, wet tongue licking her palm.

"Ick, Sparkly. Stop it. It's too early to wake up," she told her dog.

"Not if you want to be at the park by eleven," said Mr. Tanner as he pulled up the blinds, letting in the sunshine. "It's ten o'clock now."

Aly popped out of bed. They had overslept. By the time they had gotten home from the gala last night, put their fancy dresses away, and washed up, it had been past midnight.

Today Charlotte's twin brother, Caleb, was playing basketball in the park. He had asked the Sparkle Spa girls to come and cheer for his team.

"Come on, Brookester!" Aly said. "Let's move it. The girls don't know about the soccer party or the intern yet. I want to fill them in before the game."

When their dad dropped the girls off, they walked with Sparkly over to the oak tree next to the basketball court—the spot where they usually met up with the Sparkle Spa crew. Lily, Charlotte, and Caleb were already there. Charlotte was leaning against the tree, braiding Lily's hair.

Just as Aly and Brooke reached the tree, Caleb said he had to go warm up for the game. A few seconds later Sophie showed up carrying a really big bag.

Aly sent Brooke a Secret Sister Eye Message: *Should we tell them our news now?*

Brooke nodded.

"Brooke and I have two important Sparkle Spa announcements to make," she said. "Number one, the soccer team is having a Sparkle Spa party next Sunday. And number two, we're getting an intern."

"A party?" Charlotte said at the same time that Lily said, "An intern? Ouch! Charlotte, stop pulling my hair so hard."

Aly and Brooke sat down, and Aly continued. "Jenica wants to celebrate their team going to the state finals. And last night at the Businesswomen Unite gala that our mom took us to, a woman won the True Colors internship for her daughter. She starts tomorrow at the Sparkle Spa."

"Well, the soccer party should be fun," said Lily.

"But what will the intern do, Aly?" Charlotte asked. "We've already assigned all the jobs there are in the spa."

Charlotte was right.

Brooke turned to Aly. "Why don't we make a list of things to teach her?"

"And we should also make a list for the soccer party," Charlotte said. As chief operating officer of the Sparkle Spa, she would be in charge of making sure the party ran smoothly.

"Definitely," Sophie said. "I think that'll be fun. Also, after we finish, I have a present for everyone." Sophie, Brooke's best friend, was usually pretty quiet. She was a manicurist at the Sparkle Spa, and that's all she really wanted to do—she didn't want to be in charge of anything.

"That's so nice," Aly said.

"How come you didn't tell me you had a surprise?" Brooke asked.

Sophie just smiled. "I'll show you when we're done brainstorming."

After Charlotte snapped an elastic band around the bottom of Lily's braid, Lily climbed up to the lowest branch of the tree and sat dangling her legs.

Aly took her notebook and purple pen from her backpack, ready to write. Brooke lay down on the grass and put Sparkly on her chest. Sophie sprawled out on her stomach, resting her chin on her bag. "Okay, let's start with the party," Aly said.

"Manicures and pedicures," Sophie offered. "Because everyone will be expecting those."

"And we should do hair, too," Charlotte added.

"And we can make bracelets," Brooke said.

"But we've done all of that before," Aly said. "What can we do to make this party special?"

"Ask Joan to make cookies?" Lily suggested.

Brooke scratched Sparkly behind the ears. Lily tossed an acorn down on Charlotte's head. Sophie twisted two blades of grass.

"A magician?" Brooke asked.

The girls all shook their heads. "Not very spa-ish," Charlotte said.

Aly sighed. "Let's see if we can come up with something special in the next few days. In the meantime, let's switch over to our intern list."

When the girls were finished, the list looked like this:

What to Teach Our Intern
1. How to polish
   (if she doesn't know)
2. How to braid
   (if she doesn't know)
3. How to choose colors
4. How to decide on special manicures
   for special events, like the Fall Ball
   manicure

5. How to keep track of the money in the donations jar (Lily will be in charge of this because she's in charge of money)
6. How to decide which charities to donate money to
7. How to keep a schedule (Charlotte will be in charge of this)
8. How to be friendly to customers even when they annoy you

"I think that's a good list," Lily said, peering over Aly's shoulder from her spot in the tree. "Do you know anything about the intern?"

"Just that her mom's name is Carolyn Washington and she runs a company that makes shirts and hats and cups and things with people's names on them."

"I really hope she's nice," Sophie said.

"Me too," said Brooke. "But if she's not, we'll have to add that to the list: 'How to be nice.'"

Aly laughed. If you could teach a person how to be nice, she would've taught Suzy Davis ages ago. Just last week Suzy told some fourth-grade girls that the Sparkle Spa was too small and always "smelled like dog."

It was true that their spa wasn't a "big business." It was also true that Sparkly hung out at the salon a lot, but it never, ever smelled like dog. Mostly it smelled like the lavender lotion they used for manicures. And a little bit like nail polish remover.

"Are we done with the lists?" Brooke asked. "Because if we are, Sophie can give us our presents!"

Sophie opened the bag and reached in. But before she pulled anything out, she said, "You know how I drip polish on my shirt and shorts and socks and my mom gets a little bit mad?"

"I keep telling you to put a napkin or a towel in your lap," Lily said.

Sophie pulled a hot-pink apron out of the bag. Brooke's name was embroidered on it in bright yellow letters. Then she took out a purple apron with Aly's name embroidered in green. "I had aprons made for everyone, but in different colors," Sophie told the girls. She was beaming.

"These are beautiful," Brooke said, taking hers. "Thank you so much, Sophie! Pink and yellow are my two favorite colors."

"Wow!" said Aly. "I love purple and green. Thanks."

Sophie handed Lily a yellow and blue apron and a red and orange one to Charlotte.

"Where did you get these?" Charlotte said, putting hers on.

"My mom found them online," Sophie said. "A site called Custom Creations."

"No way!" Aly said. "That's the company that our intern's mom runs."

"That's got to be a good sign," Lily said, jumping down from the tree.

Sophie pulled the last apron out of the bag. It was the color of Orange You Pretty, with her own name embroidered in teal.

Brooke looked at everyone holding their aprons. "Oh my gosh! We're the colors of the rainbow sparkle pedicure!"

"Yep!" Sophie said with a laugh. "It was really my mom's idea. She just wanted me to stop ruining my clothes."

Just then Caleb came running over, calling, "Hey, Charlotte!" He was trying to spin a basketball on his finger. "It looks like Garrett isn't coming today. Any chance you want to play?"

When Caleb and Charlotte were at home, they

played basketball together. Charlotte had a great jump shot.

"Last time I took Garrett's spot, someone pushed me and I skinned my knee. Not interested in that again," she told Caleb. "Sorry."

Lily handed her apron to Sophie. "I don't mind skinned knees," she said. "I'll play."

"Cool," Caleb said. "Let's go."

"Do you think we're all set for the intern tomorrow?" Brooke asked. The girls started to walk over to watch the game.

"I think so," Aly answered. "But I don't think we're set for the soccer party. Getting to state finals is huge. We need to think of something really special for the players."

"We'll come up with something," Brooke said. "But if we don't, who knows? Maybe the intern will."

four

Cotton Candyland

On the drive to True Colors on Sunday morning, Brooke started singing, *"Today is intern day. Today is intern day. We hope she's fun and nice. And really wants to stay."* Sparkly barked along.

"Nice song," Aly said. She looked at her purple polka-dot watch. It was a little before ten. "Mom, what time is the intern coming?"

"Ten thirty," Mrs. Tanner answered. Brooke was still singing as she and Aly headed back to the Sparkle Spa.

On the way Aly made sure to ask Mrs. Howard how her new baby grandson was doing. She also checked on Jamie, one of the manicurists, who had a cold. Once in the spa, Sparkly climbed into his little bed and chewed on a toy bone.

As the girls looked at the day's schedule, Lily and Charlotte arrived.

"Schedule look good?" Charlotte asked.

"I'll start with pedicures," Aly said. "Brooke and Sophie can start with manicures, and we'll see how it goes from there. Our intern is due at ten thirty."

Lily set to work cleaning the outside of the sparkly teal strawberry-shaped jar they used to collect donations, then she checked inside it. "The jar is almost full. I'll count it at the end of the day."

A little before ten thirty, Sophie came into the spa wearing her new apron.

"You look awesome, Sophie!" Brooke squealed.

The rest of the girls put their aprons on too. Just as they were admiring how professional they all looked, Clementine Stern, their first customer for the day, showed up for her appointment and picked Cotton Candyland polish for her manicure.

Aly and Brooke wanted to be free when the intern arrived, so Sophie took her.

"Only two minutes until she gets here!" Aly announced, checking her watch again.

"Do you think she'll be someone we know?" Charlotte asked. "Or maybe she lives in a different neighborhood and goes to Dickinson or Whitman."

It was possible, Aly thought. There were three elementary schools in the area, and the mystery intern could go to any one of them.

Brooke was organizing the polish display and Aly was scrubbing a pedicure basin when Joan called,

"Girls! Mrs. Washington and her daughter are here."

Joan walked into the Sparkle Spa followed by the woman from the gala.

"Hello," Mrs. Washington said, looking right at Aly. "I hope you can teach my daughter a bit about starting a company and get her involved in and excited about business."

"I'll try," Aly answered, trying to look behind the woman for a glimpse of her daughter. But she didn't see anyone there.

The woman turned around and spoke loudly through the open door. "Suzy, come in here! What are you doing?"

Aly's stomach squinched a little. There were lots of girls named Suzy, right? It couldn't be . . .

But it was. None other than Suzy Davis marched into the Sparkle Spa, looking pretty unhappy about it in fact.

"I'm here, Mom," she said, crossing her arms in front of her.

Aly's stomach felt like it was falling all the way down to her toes. She locked eyes with Brooke, who was sending her a panicked Secret Sister Eye Message: *Suzy Davis? There's no one meaner! Now what are we going to do?*

Before the girls could react, Lily blurted out, "*You're* our intern?" then she clapped her hand over her mouth.

"You girls know each other?" Suzy's mom asked. "How nice. I'll leave you be, then. Love those aprons, by the way. From Custom Creations, right? They're marvelous! Okay, see you at four, Suzy."

And with that, Carolyn Washington and Joan left the Sparkle Spa.

Aly stared at Suzy. Suzy stared at Aly.

"But your last name is Davis," Charlotte said,

breaking the silence from her spot near the desk.

"So?" Suzy said. "My mom never changed hers because she was already a successful businesswoman when she married my dad."

"Oh," Charlotte said. "Interesting."

The way Charlotte had said it made Aly think she didn't find it very interesting at all, but Aly actually did. She wondered if she'd also want to keep the name Tanner if she was already a successful CEO when she got married.

Everyone just kept staring at one another for another minute—everyone except Sophie, that is, who was busy with Clementine's nails.

Aly couldn't believe that Suzy Davis was their intern—Suzy, the one girl at school who had been mean to her since the first day of kindergarten . . . the girl who always cut ahead of her in line every time it was pizza day at lunch . . . who'd made rabbit ears behind Charlotte's head in their second-grade school picture . . . who called Brooke "Pippi Longstocking" because of her braids (a name Brooke absolutely *hated*) . . . and who was no fan of the Sparkle Spa.

Aly took a deep breath. Maybe this internship would change things with Suzy. Maybe after she worked here, she'd stop staying mean things about the Sparkle Spa. Maybe.

Aly decided to be very professional by pretending that she'd never met Suzy—to wipe off all the old polish and start with clean fingernails, so to speak. She would act exactly like she would with a stranger, talk to her as if she were a girl she was meeting for the very first time.

"Welcome, Suzy. We're really glad to have an intern." Aly forced herself to smile. "We're looking forward to you working at the Sparkle Spa and have lots to teach you."

Suzy put her hands on her hips. "Let's get one thing straight right off the bat," she stated. "I'm *not* glad to be your intern. I *don't* want to work here. And my mom is making me do this because she wants me to run a business like her one day."

Suzy narrowed her eyes and continued, "When your mom told all the other businesswomen about—" Suzy stopped talking and shook her head. "Never mind," she said. "Anyway, I bet there's nothing you can teach me that I don't already know."

"When our mom told all the other businesswomen about what?" Brooke asked.

"Didn't you hear me? I *said* never mind," Suzy replied, plopping herself on a pillow in the jewelry-making area. "I can just sit here all day . . . even though this place is gross and smells like dog."

"It does *not* smell like dog!" Brooke screeched. She turned to everyone else. "Does it?"

"Maybe a tiny bit in Sparkly's corner," Lily said, sniffing. "But it's not a bad smell at all. Right, Sparkly?" she cooed, stroking his head. Sparkly barked and wagged his tail.

"I told you," Suzy said. "Smells like dog. Bad for business."

"But—I—you—" Brooke couldn't even get her words out.

Aly shook her head at Brooke slightly. She decided she was going to ignore anything mean that Suzy Davis did or said. She'd just act like it hadn't happened and change the subject.

Aly cleared her throat. "Do you know how to polish nails?" she asked. "We can teach you. Then you could do your mom's nails or your sister's."

Suzy glared at Aly. Then she shrugged. "Well, I don't know how to polish nails, so I guess I might as well not waste my whole day here. Fine, show me.

But you'd better be a good teacher, otherwise forget it. Also, where's *my* apron?"

Aly frowned. "We, um, didn't know you'd be coming when Sophie ordered the aprons. Sorry."

When Aly went to get Color Me Happy from the polish wall, Brooke followed. "How long is she going to be here?" she whispered.

"One week," Aly whispered back.

"That's terrible," Brooke said. "A week of terrible-ness."

Aly had no idea how she'd last a whole week with Suzy Davis in their salon. It was hard enough to last five minutes.

five

Not So Grapeful

A ly usually looked forward to Tuesdays. It was rainbow sparkle pedicure day at the salon, which meant they were always booked with the soccer team. But today she was not looking forward to Tuesday at all. Suzy Davis was coming back to the Sparkle Spa for the second day of her internship.

When the final bell rang at 3:07, Aly met up with Charlotte and Lily on the front steps of the school. Sophie and Brooke soon joined them.

"Do we have to wait for Suzy?" Brooke asked.

Aly sighed. "I think so."

Every time Aly thought about Suzy in the salon, she also thought about how Suzy had accidentally-on-purpose poured chocolate milk on her white leggings in third grade. On school picture day. And how Suzy had come into the Sparkle Spa demanding that someone fix her broken nail when the day was already booked, then had screamed and yelled when no one could do it right away. She really was the pits.

A few minutes later Suzy came out of school with her younger sister, Heather, and Heather's friend Jayden.

"What are you doing here?" Suzy asked Aly. "Shouldn't you be at the Sparkle Spa?"

"We were waiting for you," Brooke told her. "What took you so long?"

Suzy pointed to a red car in front of the school.

"We were waiting inside for our babysitter. She's going to take me to the spa. I don't know why you waited for me—I didn't say I was going to walk there with you."

"But . . . but . . . ," Brooke sputtered.

"It's okay," Aly said. "See you at the salon, Suzy."

The girls started walking while Suzy, Heather, and Jayden climbed into the red car.

"She makes me so mad! Heather better not turn into Suzy," Brooke fumed.

"I just don't understand," Charlotte added, pumping her elbows back and forth. "Doesn't she want to be friends?"

Sophie wiped a strand of hair out of her eye. "I don't think she does. Maybe we should try harder to be friends with her."

Brooke picked up her racewalking speed. "I am *not* trying harder with her," she huffed.

"Hey, wait," Lily said, trying to catch up to her. "Slow down!"

Aly thought maybe Sophie was right. Then again, maybe she wasn't.

When the girls reached the salon, the babysitter's car was parked out front.

"You girls are a little late today," Mom said when they walked through the front door. "Is everything okay?"

"Well—" Brooke started, but Aly cut her off with one of their secret looks.

"Everything's fine," she said.

"Okay. Pretzels and juice are back in the Sparkle Spa for you. And don't forget your homework."

"We never do, Mrs. Tanner," Charlotte said.

Mom smiled. "Just a reminder."

The girls expected to find Suzy in the back room, but she wasn't there.

"I wonder where she is," Lily said. "Maybe she's sitting in the car?"

"She better come in soon. We need to prep her before the soccer players get here," Aly said.

Just as the girls were finishing their homework, Suzy showed up. "What are you doing? Why aren't you giving manicures?" she asked.

"Everyone has to finish their homework before we open the salon," Brooke explained. "It's a rule. A Sparkle Spa rule."

"Well, everyone except for me, because I'm not doing it," Suzy said. "I don't do my homework until after dinner. And," she added, looking at the bag of open pretzels on the break table, "I already had a better snack than that in the car. I'm ready to start polishing."

Charlotte looked alarmed. Aly cleared her throat. "Before you can be a manicurist, I need to see how well you do—have you been practicing what we went over on Sunday? You can polish my nails. Toes or fingers, you pick—either one is fine."

When Suzy didn't answer right away, Aly stood still and crossed her arms. Charlotte did the same. Then Brooke. They all stared at Suzy.

Suzy rolled her eyes. "Fine," she said. She grabbed a bottle of Not So Grapeful off the polish shelf and sat down at one of the manicure stations. "I'm ready, Aly. Let's go."

Bethany and Mia, two of the soccer players, were booked first. Brooke and Sophie turned on the water to fill the pedicure basins as the girls took their seats.

"Can you believe we made it to states?" Mia said as she excitedly wiggled her toes in the water. "Please make my pedicure extra sparkly and extra powerful today so we can take the whole championship!"

"That's ridiculous," Suzy muttered under her breath.

"Shhh," Aly whispered to her.

"I can believe you guys made it," Lily said from her spot near the donations jar. "You're awesome—undefeated all season!"

Bethany laughed. "It's true. We are."

Charlotte glanced at the wall calendar. "Jenica's due in next," she announced. "And Valentina."

"Jenica's here!" Jenica said from the door.

"And Valentina, too," Valentina said. "Oh, do you have a new manicurist?" she asked as she and Jenica made their way to the couch to wait.

"Hi," Suzy said, introducing herself. "I'm Suzy Davis. I work here now too."

"Cool!" Valentina said.

"She's an intern," Aly clarified. "Just for this week. Her mom wants her to learn about running a business."

Aly thought Suzy was about to hiss at her.

"Speaking of running things," Jenica said, "did you come up with any great ideas for the soccer party?"

Suzy stopped polishing Aly's nails for a second.

"Well," Aly said, "we were thinking manicures and pedicures and braids and bracelets and pizza and cookies." She still wished they'd come up with something else. "And, um, something else exciting."

Jenica nodded. "What's the other exciting thing going to be?"

"We're still working on that," Charlotte said.

Suzy put down the bottle of polish. "It could be a pool party," she said. "My house has a really big pool, and my parents keep it heated year-round."

"I love pool parties," Valentina said.

"It can't be a pool party," Brooke snapped. "It's a *spa* party. How would we get all of our spa supplies to a pool?"

"In a suitcase?" Bethany suggested.

Aly wasn't sure what to say. It seemed like the team wanted a pool party. But Brooke was right. And also, this wasn't *Suzy's* salon. She wasn't allowed to make the plans.

"We'll talk about it," Aly said.

"Okay." Jenica smiled. "I know you'll make the party awesome."

Suzy had just one more nail to polish. "So," she said, "am I approved?"

Aly looked at her fingers. She checked for polish on her skin and streaks on her nails, but the manicure was almost perfect. Aly couldn't believe it. On Sunday, when Suzy had polished Charlotte's nails, she wasn't that good. Suzy must have practiced a lot in the last couple of days. There was no reason Aly couldn't make Suzy a manicurist.

"You're approved," she told Suzy.

Suzy jumped up from the chair.

"What?" asked Brooke. She walked over to her sister and held up Aly's hands, inspecting them for a long time.

"So?" Suzy asked.

"You must have practiced a ton," Brooke said.

Suzy shrugged. "Whatever, it's just polishing. It's not *that* hard."

Brooke's faced flushed. She was about to yell when Sophie said, "Well, I'm impressed. It took me a lot longer to learn."

"So who do I get to do first?" Suzy asked.

"She can polish my nails while I wait for a pedicure chair to open up," Valentina offered.

"I'll help you pick out a nail color if you want," Lily told her.

"You know," Suzy said, sitting down at the second manicure station, "I can give you all some tips about how I do manicures."

And that's when Brooke lost it. "*We* are the experts," she said. "And this is *our* salon. You're lucky you're here."

Aly raised her eyebrows at Brooke, who immediately closed her mouth.

"Your loss," Suzy replied. "Come on, Valentina. I'll give you the best manicure you've ever had in your life. Way better than the ones you usually get here."

Aly did not like Suzy. And she did not like how Suzy was trying to take charge of everything. But she was curious: What manicure tips *did* Suzy have that she and Brooke didn't know?

Six

Rainbow Bright

I never thought I'd be happy we're *not* open on Wednesday," Brooke said.

She and Aly were stretched out on the floor pillows in the Sparkle Spa doing their homework, glad that no one was there to bother them, especially Suzy.

"I know," Aly said as she put her finger on her spot in *The Master Puppeteer*, her reading homework for language arts. "Having Suzy Davis as our intern is the worst thing that ever happened to this place."

Brooke popped a carrot into her mouth. "At least

she'll be gone after this weekend." She looked at her math sheet. "If Andrew has four cookies and Sarah has three cookies and they give Jason two cookies, how many cookies do Andrew and Sarah have left?"

"Are you asking me to do your homework for you?" Aly asked her sister. Brooke sometimes tried to get away with that.

"Help," Brooke said. "I'm asking for help."

Aly stood up and grabbed seven bottles of nail polish. She put them down in front of Brooke. "Okay, give Andrew four bottles of polish," she said.

Brooke put four bottles in a group on her right.

"Now give Sarah three, next to Andrew's."

Brooke moved the other polishes over, so all seven were grouped together.

"Now take two of those polishes and give them to Jason."

Brooke took two of the bottles and put them on her left side.

"Now count the ones on your right," Aly told her as she sat back down, holding her book.

"Five?" Brooke asked.

Aly grinned.

"That was so cool!" Brooke said. She went to the polish wall, took down more bottles, and finished her homework quickly and quietly while Aly continued reading.

"How's it going in here?" Joan asked. "I don't know what's making me so thirsty today, but I need another bottle of water from the fridge."

"Aly made my homework easier with nail polish," Brooke reported.

"Glad to hear it," Joan said, sitting on the floor next to the girls. "So, how's the intern working out?"

Brooke was about to spew out their long list of

complaints, but Aly silenced her with a look. She didn't want Joan and Mom to think they couldn't handle problems like real businesswomen.

"I think her mom wants her to be an intern more than she does. But we're still teaching her," Aly said. "We're making the best of it."

Joan ruffled Aly's hair. "You girls always do," she said. "By the way, I have some new cookies I want you to test out. Brookie, they're in my bag in the closet in a container."

Brooke jumped up and ran to the closet. Cookies were her favorite. Especially Joan's.

When Brooke handed Joan her bag, she pulled out two rainbow-colored cookies that looked like the twisty tops of soft-serve ice cream covered in glitter. They reminded Aly of Rainbow Bright nail polish, which had about a million different sparkly colors in it.

"Sparkles you can eat?" Brooke asked, wide-eyed.

Joan nodded solemnly. "These cookies are called Unicorn Goop," she said.

Aly and Brooke burst out laughing.

"Goop?" Brooke gasped.

Joan was laughing now too. "Taste them," she said. "They don't taste like goop, I promise."

The cookies were sweet and lemony and crisp on the outside. "Mmm." Aly smacked her lips. "I like the lemony part."

"I think I can taste the sparkles," Brooke said. "They're like rainbows in my mouth!"

"So a thumbs-up?" Joan asked.

Aly nodded. "Except for the name."

"Wait!" Brooke said. "These would be perfect for the soccer team! Joan, could you make them for a spa party we're having this Sunday?"

"I'd be happy to," she said, standing up. "But how about if you girls help me? Tomorrow afternoon I'm going to use some of the time I bought in the Sweet Treats kitchen at the auction. If you come with me, we can make Unicorn Goop together."

"Joan, can't we call them Unicorn Treats?" Aly asked.

Joan smiled. "Sure, why not?" Then she checked her watch. "I have to get ready for Mrs. Bass. She'll be here in a minute or two. When you girls are done in here, the True Colors polish display needs organizing. And the magazines need restacking."

"We're on it," Aly said. "No problem."

When Joan had returned to the main salon, Brooke told her sister, "Well, at least Suzy didn't come up with Unicorn Treats for the soccer party. They'll be our surprise."

Aly sighed. "I guess," she said. "But I still think we need something more."

✳　✳　✳　✳　✳

After school on Thursday the girls walked to Sweet Treats Kitchen & Bakery instead of True Colors. Joan was already there, waiting for them with all of the Unicorn Treats ingredients laid out on the counter.

"Look who else is here," Joan said as the girls walked in.

It was Isaac—the photographer the girls had met when they took part in Adoption Day at the Paws for Love animal shelter a while back.

"Hi, Isaac," Aly said.

"Hi, Isaac," Brooke echoed.

"Nice to see you girls again," he said. "Joan asked me to take some pictures for her baking website, so just pretend I'm not here. We're going for a natural look."

Isaac clicked away, photographing the girls from all different angles.

Joan, Aly, and Brooke measured and mixed and probably made a little bit more of a mess than they should have. Isaac took pictures the whole time.

After the cookies went into the oven, Isaac said, "Okay, ladies. Big smiles in front of the oven."

Aly and Brooke stood on either side of Joan with their arms around her waist.

Isaac clicked.

And so did an idea in Aly's head.

Walking home from Sweet Treats, Aly told Brooke her idea.

"We can do photo shoots at the soccer party," she explained. "Remember Katie Heller's sixth-grade graduation party? She had a Polaroid camera, and we all got to take home instant photographs that day."

"I still have that picture on my bulletin board," Brooke answered. "But, Aly, how are we going to get an instant camera in time for Sunday?"

$\mathcal{S}$even
Orange You Happy?

$\mathbf{A}$ly was at lunch with Charlotte and Lily when she saw Brooke waving at her from the door of the cafeteria.

"I'll be right back," Aly told her friends.

"Everything okay?" she asked Brooke when she got to the door.

"No. There's an SSE—a Sparkle Spa Emergency: Sophie's sick." Brooke frowned. "She came to school this morning but got a fever. She had to go home right before lunch. What are we going to do for all of her customers at the Sparkle Spa?"

Aly closed her eyes and tried to think. "Well, you and I could just wiggle our schedules around and each do more people . . ."

Brooke tugged on her braid. "Are you sure people won't get mad about having to wait or be rescheduled? It is a school day, you know. Kids have homework and after-school stuff."

Brooke was right. Customers wouldn't be happy. It was too bad Charlotte and Lily weren't interested in being manicurists. Oh no. That left only . . .

"Suzy Davis," Aly said.

Brooke groaned. But then she said, "You're right. Suzy Davis. But I really don't like that Suzy Davis is the answer to our problem."

"Wait a minute. What are you doing out of class?" Aly asked. The third graders were usually finished with recess by the time the fifth graders had lunch. Brooke should've been back in class by now.

"Bathroom pass," Brooke said, holding up a

wooden circle dangling from a piece of yarn. "I have to go back, though."

"Okay, see you after school. I'll go find Suzy now and tell her the news."

Most of the fifth graders had finished lunch and had gone outside. Aly and Charlotte tracked Suzy down on the bench near the monkey bars. She was scribbling something in a notebook, but the minute she saw the girls coming, she snapped it closed.

"So we're in a bit of a bind," Aly told Suzy, "and we really need help." She took a deep breath. "It would be really great if you could come into the salon right after school and take all of Sophie's clients for us today."

"What if I don't want to?" she said.

"Suzy!" Charlotte almost yelled. "Can you be nice for one afternoon and help us out?"

Suzy scrunched up her mouth for a moment. "How about this: If I do help you pick up the slack today, you have to listen to my ideas for improvements to your salon."

"Suzy!" Charlotte really did yell this time.

But Aly knew that they needed Suzy's cooperation today. Badly. So she nodded and said, "We'll listen. That doesn't mean we'll do everything you suggest, but we'll listen."

"Okay," Suzy answered. "Fine. I'll fill in for Sophie today." Then, all of a sudden, Suzy stood up on the bench. "Attention, everyone!" she announced to the whole schoolyard. "I'll be a full-time manicurist at the Sparkle Spa today. If you come by and ask for me, you'll get a free cupcake too!"

Free cupcakes! Aly couldn't believe what she was hearing. She jumped up on the bench next to Suzy. "You will *not* get a free cupcake!" she yelled out. "And Suzy is pretty much all booked up for the afternoon anyway!"

Suzy glared at Aly.

Aly glared back at Suzy.

"I was going to bring the cupcakes myself," Suzy said.

Aly ran her fingers through her hair. "It's not a bad idea, Suzy, but you have to *ask* first. You're just our intern there—you're not a permanent team member. And even permanent team members have to ask me and Brooke."

Suzy jumped off the bench, grabbed her notebook, and stomped away.

"See you later, Suzy!" Charlotte called after her.

Aly climbed down from the bench. "I hope she shows up at the spa," she muttered.

"Me too," Charlotte said. "Me too."

The minute Suzy walked through the Sparkle Spa door, she took over.

"First of all," Suzy began as she laid out polish

remover and an emery board at the manicure station she was clearly claiming as her own for the day, "you really need a third manicure station and a third pedicure chair in here. That way, all of the polishers you have on staff now can be working at the same time, taking more customers, even if they all want just manicures or just pedicures."

Suzy had a point. But Aly didn't think they'd be able to convince their mom to buy them more stations. The ones they had now were hand-me-downs from True Colors.

"We'll talk to our mom about it." Aly just wanted to keep Suzy happy until all their appointments for today were taken care of.

"And about the soccer party this weekend . . . ," Suzy started.

"Yeah, we have to get decorations," Brooke said. "I was thinking sparkly streamers with paper soccer balls hanging off of them."

"Where are you going to get paper soccer balls?" Suzy asked, filing a third grader's nails.

"I'll draw them," Brooke told her. She turned on the warm water to fill a pedicure basin for her next appointment, a sixth grader named Uma.

"Brooke's a really good artist," Charlotte said.

"Well, it won't look professional," Suzy said, "no matter how good an artist she is. I'm just saying."

Aly tucked her hair behind her ears. She didn't like to admit it, but Suzy Davis was right about a lot of things. As far as Aly was concerned, though, since Brooke *was* a good artist, who really cared if her soccer balls looked professional or not?

Hannah Goodman, a fourth grader from Auden, walked in. Aly sat down at the second manicure station to do her nails.

"Is there a Color of the Week?" Hannah asked.

"It's Orange You Happy," Brooke said.

"That's another thing," Suzy said. "What's the point of the Color of the Week? Does anyone actually care?"

Charlotte opened her mouth, but she ended up throwing her arms in the air and shaking her head.

Aly didn't know how Suzy did it, but now she was making customers feel bad about liking the Color of the Week.

Suzy was just about done with her first manicure when Anjuli, the goalie for the soccer team, walked in and took Power to the Sparkle off the display wall. Charlotte pointed her toward Suzy.

"I just need a touch-up," she said. "My index finger is chipped, and I want to make sure I have as much sparkle power as possible for the state championship tomorrow."

Suzy checked Anjuli's nails. "I can just redo them all," she said. "So it's fresh."

"Okay," Anjuli said. "I have time."

While Suzy removed Anjuli's old polish, Anjuli said, "I'm really excited about the spa party on Sunday. Have you come up with a cool surprise yet?"

"We did," Aly said.

"But we're keeping it a secret," Brooke added.

"Even from me?" Charlotte asked as she looked over the schedule.

"We'll tell you later, Char," Aly said. "We don't want to give away the surprise."

"What about me?" Suzy asked. "I work here too now, you know."

Aly hesitated. She didn't want to tell Suzy anything she didn't have to. And what if she made fun of their idea?

"You're only here one more day," Brooke reminded her.

For once, Suzy didn't have a reply. But that only lasted a moment. "Anjuli, don't *you* think it should

72

be a pool party?" She took the last bit of polish off Anjuli's pinkie.

Anjuli shrugged. "Pool parties are fun."

"No, they're not," Brooke huffed.

Did Suzy just smile? Aly asked herself. She wasn't sure why, but it made her a little nervous.

"Yes, they are," Suzy said. Then she screeched, "*Oops!* I got polish on my leg."

"You can get it off with some remover," Aly said. "It's a good thing it was your leg and not your shorts."

"Actually," Suzy said, "I think I can turn it into a flower."

Anjuli watched as Suzy made petals and a stem with nail polish on her leg.

"That's pretty cool," Anjuli said. "Can you make me one too? Maybe on my arm?"

"Sure," Suzy said. "It's easy."

"Wait," Aly said. "I'm not sure if that's allowed. I should ask my mom first."

"Isn't this *your* salon?" Suzy asked.

Aly looked at Brooke. Brooke looked at Aly.

"Fine," Brooke said. "It's our salon. And we say it's okay to paint on people with nail polish."

After Anjuli, Suzy polished a Red Between the Lines heart on Parker Reed's wrist, two Lemon Aid stars on Laurel Forte's left ankle, and an All That Glitters moon on Heidi Yeh's knee. She was just about to paint a butterfly on Karina Montoya's upper arm when Mrs. Tanner came through the door.

"Hi, girls," she said. But then she stopped in her tracks when she saw Suzy holding Karina's arm. "Aly and Brooke, may I see you in True Colors, please?"

The girls quickly followed their mother out the door.

"What's going on in there?" she asked quietly.

"Nail polish is *not* meant to be painted on skin. And more than that, it's a waste of money to use nail polish for that purpose. If you want to add body art to your salon, let's talk about the products that are made for that reason."

Aly was staring at the wood grains on the floor. "I'm sorry," she said.

"Aly?" Mom said, lifting her daughter's chin up with her finger.

"We won't do it again," Aly said, a little louder.

"It wasn't even our *fault!*" Brooke complained, pushing her glasses up her nose. "And Aly *wanted* to ask you, she even said—"

Aly gave Brooke a Secret Sister Eye Message: *Shhh.*

In the end, she and Brooke were in charge of the salon and had to take responsibility for everything that happened there.

"Hmm?" Mom prompted. "She said what?"

"It's nothing, Mom. You're right," Aly said. "We should have known better. When we're home later, we can talk about body art."

"Okay," Mom said, smoothing Brooke's hair back. "Make sure those girls take the polish off their skin before they leave. I don't want them walking out of here like that."

Once Mom left, Brooke turned to Aly and whispered, "Now Suzy even got *us* in trouble!"

As they walked back into the Sparkle Spa, Aly felt pretty sure that they'd gotten themselves in trouble. Suzy Davis had just helped.

Once the afternoon rush was over, Brooke started putting the polish bottles back on the display and Lily counted the donations before she left for the day.

"So, for my internship," Suzy said while she puffed

up the floor pillows, "I'm curious: What do you ask each customer who wants their nails done—what information do you get?"

Aly was surprised at Suzy's interest, but maybe she was trying to make up for the way she'd been acting all week. Charlotte looked surprised too. "Well," she answered, "we get their name, what services they want, what time they want to come, and their phone number—in case we have to cancel or change their appointment."

"And where do you store the old schedules once they're done?"

"In that drawer," Charlotte told her, pointing to one at the bottom of the desk. "We like to see how many new people we get each week. One day, when it's not so busy, I'm going to make a list of all of our clients."

"That's a good plan," Suzy said.

Aly started to grow suspicious. This was the first time since Suzy began her internship that she'd said something positive about the salon.

An alarm beeped on Charlotte's watch. "I have to go," she said. "My mom will be outside soon. We have to pick up Caleb at karate and can't be late." Charlotte hugged Aly good-bye.

"I'll call you later, about the soccer surprise," Aly whispered in her ear.

Sparkly whined in his corner.

"I think he needs to go out," Brooke said, petting his head.

"Want to come with us to walk him?" Aly asked Suzy, secretly hoping that she'd just go home.

"My babysitter's coming to pick me up in five minutes, so I should probably stay. But I'll see you on Sunday."

"Okay," Aly said. "See you on Sunday."

Brooke clipped Sparkly's leash on his collar, and they led him outside.

"Was Suzy being extra weird just now?" Brooke asked.

"I know. She has to be up to something, but what could it be? I don't know what to think about her," Aly answered.

"At least her internship is up after the weekend. Then she'll be gone for good," Brooke said.

Sparkly raced ahead, and Aly and Brooke had to run to keep up with him.

"She'll never be gone for good," Aly said. "She goes to Auden. She'll be with us forever."

eight
Yellow Giggles

When Aly and Brooke returned from walking Sparkly, Suzy Davis was gone. But before she'd left, Suzy had made some changes to the Sparkle Spa. She'd rearranged the furniture so that the jewelry-making area was now about two feet farther to the left, which created more space between the manicure stations. In that space, she'd moved the desk chair and put ten different nail polish colors on it.

"What is *that*?" Brooke asked. "And what happened to our waiting area?"

"This has Suzy Davis written all over it," Aly replied as she started gathering their things together to leave for the evening.

Brooke marched over and put everything back where it belonged. "I can't believe her!"

"You know," Aly said, "I bet Suzy would actually be good at being in charge somewhere. She's just not very good at *not* being in charge."

"We've got more important things to worry about," Brooke answered. "Getting everything ready for the soccer party and getting a camera for our photo shoots."

Finding a Polaroid camera wasn't as easy as Aly had thought it would be. The local camera store didn't carry them, and it was way too late to order one online. Plus, Polaroid cameras—and their film— were expensive. More than the thirty-seven dollars

and fifty-nine cents Lily had counted in the strawberry donation jar that afternoon.

Brooke hadn't come up with one of her creative
solutions to this problem yet, so at dinner that night,
she barely touched her meal.

"What's wrong, Brooke?" Dad asked. "Chicken
and rice is one of your favorites."

Aly answered for her. "We need a camera for
Sunday's Sparkle Spa soccer party. Not only haven't
we found one, but even if we did, we wouldn't have
enough money to buy it," Aly told their parents. "And
that was going to be our big surprise—a Polaroid
photo shoot. Now we have to come up with a whole
new idea all over again."

"When we're finished eating," Dad said, "let's
check the attic. I have a feeling there might be something up there you can use."

"The attic?" Aly groaned. "We'll never find a
camera up there that works."

Taking one last bite of chicken, Brooke added, "Aly's right, Dad. The attic is just filled with old junk."

The attic in the Tanner house had become the place where everything the family didn't use anymore had found a home. It was filled with old stacked boxes labeled everything from BABY CLOTHES: 6–9 MONTHS and MARK'S BUSINESS SCHOOL BOOKS and GRANDMA BETTY'S CHINA to ALY'S SCHOOLWORK: 1ST–3RD GRADE and BROOKE'S KINDERGARTEN ARTWORK.

Of course, that's also where the girls had found a lot of the furnishings for the Sparkle Spa—including the teal strawberry jar, which their mother had made when she was in art school, and the pictures they'd hung on the walls.

"You really think there's a camera up here?" Aly asked after she and Brooke had climbed up the rickety ladder behind Dad.

"Help me look for the box marked 'old apartment,' will you?" Dad asked. "I think it's over there."

"Old apartment?" asked Brooke, peeking underneath a dusty quilt. "What's that?"

Dad leaned against a dresser and smiled. "It's everything left over from the first apartment your mom and I lived in together right after we got married. She wanted to throw out anything we didn't need. But I'm a saver. I packed most of my things away and stored the boxes up here. If I remember correctly, I'm pretty sure there's a Polaroid camera in that box."

Aly had wandered to the other side of the attic and found a pile of boxes behind a wobbly bookshelf. "Here it is! The box from the old apartment!"

Dad used a key from his key ring to slit open the sealed box. Aly and Brooke peered over his shoulder. He took out a broken flashlight, a rolled-up welcome mat, and a smaller box filled with letters.

Underneath all that there was another square box.

"The Polaroid!" he said. Then he rummaged around a bit more. "And film. I knew it!"

He opened a package of film and loaded it into the camera. "I doubt the film will still work. But it was sealed up this whole time, so let's try. Smile!" he said to the girls.

He clicked a button, a flash went off, and a few seconds later a grayish piece of paper came out of the camera.

"The picture is going to develop. Watch," Dad told them.

Slowly, the shiny gray paper started looking not so gray anymore. Aly and Brooke saw ghosts of themselves start taking shape on the paper, and then there they were! The detail wasn't great, and neither was the color, but it was definitely them.

"Whoa!" Brooke was grinning. "Awesome. Just like at Katie Heller's party! It smells funny, doesn't it?"

"It's certainly different from the kind of digital pictures we take now. We just need to find newer film. I can drive out to the mall tomorrow and check a few stores," Dad said. "So do you think this will work for the soccer party, Aly?"

"I think so," she said, smiling.

The three Tanners climbed down from the attic, Dad carrying the camera and the three boxes of film he'd found.

Brooke was chattering away a mile a minute. "This is going to be so, so cool," she was saying. "The camera's like magic. Maybe we should tell everyone it's magical. That would be so funny. But I don't know if anyone would believe us."

Aly couldn't help but laugh. When Brooke was excited about something, she couldn't stop her mouth from going and going and going.

* * * * *

On Saturday, Sophie was still sick. But later that afternoon Charlotte and Lily came over to help with the party decorations. Brooke and Aly had bought a big roll of brown paper that was taller than Brooke. The girls decided on three different backgrounds for the photo booth: an ocean, a mountain, and a starry sky.

Brooke had already finished outlining the scenes, and the other three girls were coloring them in as Brooke had instructed them.

"This is going to be so neat," Charlotte said. "Maybe, for practice, we should take our pictures in front of the backgrounds with your dad's camera. You know, to see how they come out."

Brooke shook her head. "We can't waste the film. My dad found some more in a small camera shop i Waltham this morning, but we still have to save Maybe once the party is over we can take a few tures of ourselves."

"Or maybe we can take *one* practice shot tomorrow before the party," Aly suggested. "How does that sound, Brooke?"

Brooke thought about it. "We'll see."

"So, Charlotte," Aly said, "let's go over the rest of the plans for the party."

Charlotte stopped coloring. "Okay, well, we'll have four stations running at the same time. Aly, you'll do pedicures, Brooke will take care of the manicures, I'll do braids, and Lily can take the pictures. The players can be in charge of beading bracelets themselves. And we'll set up the pizza and the cookies on the table at the start of the party so everyone can eat whenever they want."

It all sounded good to Aly, but then she remembered: Suzy Davis. "What about a job for Suzy?" Aly asked. "She's still our intern for one more day, and we need to give her a party assignment."

Charlotte groaned. "How about if she's in charge of the jewelry station, then? Or helping pick out polish colors?"

Aly had a feeling Suzy wasn't going to like either one of those jobs. "Maybe she can do pedicures with me. They take a little longer than manicures, so it might be good to have two people."

"If you want the help, sure," Charlotte said.

By the end of the day, the girls were as ready as they could be for tomorrow. Part of Aly didn't care if Suzy went along with all the arrangements or not. The party wasn't about Suzy. And Aly planned to keep it that way.

nine

Not Number Blue

"Isn't Suzy supposed to be here by now?" Lily grunted.

It was ten thirty on Sunday, a half hour before the Auden Angels' soccer spa party was set to begin. Lily was standing on one of the pedicure chairs, taping a streamer to the wall.

"Are you really complaining because she's not?" Charlotte asked her.

"It would just be easier with more of us here to help," Lily answered. "With Sophie still not feeling well, we really need Suzy today."

Aly had been stacking containers of Unicorn Treats on the table, but now she walked over to help Lily. She climbed onto the second pedicure chair and took the other side of the streamer. "How's this?" she asked, holding her end up against the wall. "Are we even?"

Brooke was unrolling the photograph backgrounds on the floor and looked up. "A smidge higher, Aly," she said.

"Now?" she asked.

"Perfect," Brooke said.

The little paper soccer balls Brooke had made were dangling from the streamers, floating back and forth in the breeze from the air vents.

"Should we hang the backgrounds up now?" Brooke asked, holding up the first one. "I was thinking we could do it behind the jewelry station." That seemed to be the only place in the spa with any open wall space.

"Sounds good," Charlotte told her, and she headed over with a roll of masking tape to help.

Ten minutes later the Sparkle Spa was transformed. "It looks beautiful in here," Brooke said. "I think it's okay if we take just one sample picture in front of one the backgrounds so everyone knows what to do."

Lily picked up the camera. "The three of you stand together, and I'll take the photo."

"Say 'sparkle'!" Lily said.

"Sparkle!" Aly, Brooke, and Charlotte repeated. And just like magic, the picture developed in front of their eyes.

"Girls," Mrs. Tanner said, walking into the spa, "you've done a wonderful job. It looks great in here. Nice photo booth too."

"We could make one for True Colors," Brooke offered.

Mom laughed. "Thanks, Brookie, I'll let you know. What time is your party starting?"

Aly looked at her watch: 11:03. "Um," she said, "three minutes ago? I wonder where everyone is."

"There might be traffic," Mom said reassuringly. "But where's Carolyn's daughter? Isn't today her last day with you girls?"

"We're not sure," Aly told her mom. "We were just going to call her."

"Well, have a super party. I'll send the pizza back when it arrives." Mom smiled and left.

"It's kind of weird that no one's here yet, right?" Lily wondered.

Brooke said, "Jenica's always early. Maybe Mom's right about a traffic jam."

Aly paced back and forth. "There's a problem about calling Suzy. I don't know her number."

"I bet she's in our records. Don't forget, she

and Heather have been customers here," Charlotte reminded them. She walked over to the desk.

But when she opened the bottom drawer, she gasped. "Our records are gone!"

Brooke ran over. "What?" she squealed. "It's empty! The whole drawer's empty! Who would take our records?"

All at once, everyone knew exactly who would take their records.

Suzy Davis.

Aly picked up the portable phone from True Colors that her mother let the girls keep in the spa and closed her eyes. "Jenica got a cell phone for her birthday this year. I'm trying to remember her number. . . ."

She wasn't sure if she was dialing correctly, but after a couple of rings Jenica picked up.

"Hey, Aly!" she said. Aly could hear chattering and laughter in the background. "Where are you guys? Suzy said you were coming, but you're late. And guess what? We won yesterday."

Aly felt the blood drain out of her face. "Uh . . . um . . . Congratulations, Jenica! That's awesome. But, wait, you're *where*?" she asked.

"At Suzy's," Jenica answered. "She called everyone last night and explained that the party was being moved to her house—that the big surprise was that it was going to be a combination pool party and spa party. So we're all here!"

Aly swallowed hard. She couldn't let Jenica or any other customer know that there was a problem at the Sparkle Spa. A pretty big one. "Sorry," she said. "We, um, got a little lost. Can you tell me the address again?"

Jenica gave her the information, and Aly hung up the phone, fighting back tears. Suzy had not only stolen their customer files, but she'd hijacked their soccer spa party!

Aly took a deep breath. "So . . . ," she told everyone, "they're all at Suzy Davis's house."

"*What?!*" Brooke screamed. "Are you kidding?"

"She is the absolute worst," Lily added, plopping down onto a pillow. "What are we going to do? We have a whole party set up here and no one's coming to it."

Aly tried to stay calm. That's what you had to do when you were in charge. No matter what, you had to come up with a plan. What *could* they do? They couldn't get the party to come back to the spa—not at this point.

But maybe, just maybe . . .

Turning to the girls, Aly stood up tall and announced, "This is what we're going to do. I got Suzy's address from Jenica. Charlotte, call the pizza place and have them deliver our order to Suzy's instead. Lily, pack up the cookies. Brooke, you and I will pack up all of the nail supplies and roll up the photo backdrops. If we can't have the party here, we're going to take the party to Suzy's. Suzy didn't tell the team that she'd hijacked the party, so we can just pretend like this was the plan all along."

"What about my streamers?" Brooke asked. "With all the soccer balls on them?"

"Well take those, too," Aly said. "And the beads and the string also. Quick, let's go."

The girls were collecting all the supplies in bags and boxes when Mom poked her head back in the Sparkle Spa. "What's happening in here?" she asked.

"Suzy Davis stole our party!" Brooke told her. "And our customer records! And we're going to get them back!"

"*What?*" Mom said, stepping into the spa.

"We can't be one hundred percent sure about the customer files, but the whole soccer team is at her house," Aly informed her mom. "So we're moving the party to Suzy's. Can you take us?"

"Suzy came here to learn how to run a business and then tried to take over yours?" Mom did not look happy. "Oh, I can take you, all right," she said. "And I'm going to have a talk with Suzy's mother when we get there."

The girls marched out of the salon with Mrs. Tanner leading the way. "Joan, I need you to rearrange the schedule so my next two appointments are taken care of," she said. "The girls and I have some important business to attend to right away."

"Is everything okay?" Joan asked.

"It will be," Mom said. "Let's go, girls."

They all squished into Mom's car with cookies and streamers and backdrops on their laps.

Suzy Davis had totally taken the Sparkle Spa by surprise.

Now it was time to surprise Suzy.

ten

Celegrape Good Times

Mom parked the car in the Davises' driveway and headed straight for the front door.

"Whoa," Brooke said. "This house is enormous."

Aly stopped to look. *Wow.* It *was* huge. Aly counted three floors. To the side of the house, it looked like there was a tennis court with the pool behind that.

"They're here!" Aly heard Jenica call from the backyard, and then Maxie and Joelle came running around the side of the house to greet them.

"What color polishes did you bring? Did you remember Under the Sea?" Maxie asked excitedly.

"We want the most partyish polishes you have," Joelle added.

"We brought a bunch," Aly said. "But we need to get set up first. Where's Suzy?"

"In the kitchen, I think," Joelle said. "The pizza came just before you did."

"Thanks," Aly said. "We'll let you know when everything's ready."

Aly headed into the house with Brooke, Charlotte, and Lily behind her. The door was open, so she walked right in and found her mom having a conversation with Suzy's mom in the front hall.

"I had no idea," Suzy's mom was saying. "I'm so sorry. I'll talk to her."

"I'd appreciate that, Carolyn. You know how hard it is for women in business. We're supposed to stick together, not undermine each other. I've taught my girls about teamwork."

"I'll talk to her," Suzy's mom said again.

"I'm so tempted to take my daughters and their friends—and their customers—back to the salon," Mrs. Tanner continued, "but they seem to be having fun here, so I'll let them stay. But if Suzy doesn't hand over their customer files today, I don't think I want her back at the salon. At least not for a while."

Mom turned around then and saw the girls standing there. "I'll be back for you in a few hours," she said. "Make this party great."

An embarrassed look crossed Suzy's mom's face. "The kitchen's that way," she said to the girls, pointing. "Please tell Suzy I need to see her out here."

"Thanks, Mrs. Washington," Aly answered. "We will."

Suzy squealed when Brooke and Aly entered the

kitchen. "Isn't this great? Everyone's having the best time! Thanks for sending over the pizza. I had to pay for it from my allowance, so if you have the money . . ."

"Your mom wants to see you out there," Brooke said, pointing a thumb toward the hallway.

Suzy's smile turned to a frown. "What did you say to her?" she asked.

"*We* didn't say anything," Aly told her. "Our mom did."

Suzy closed her eyes for a second. Then her face looked like it usually did: bored. "Whatever," she said. "I see you brought stuff. The soccer girls probably won't want to do whatever it is anyway, since a pool is cooler than any of that." And then she walked out of the kitchen into the hallway.

"I don't like this," Lily said.

"Me neither," Aly said, "but we have a job to do. So let's get going."

✳ ✳ ✳ ✳ ✳

Blue cereal bowls, rolls of paper towels, the round kitchen table, four chairs, the granite counters—the girls used everything they could to set up a makeshift salon.

While they were setting up, they tried to ignore the conversation going on in the hallway. But it was hard to ignore. Suzy's mom was speaking firmly: "I bought this for you so that you could learn how to run a business with kids your own age. What happened?"

The girls weren't sure, but they thought they heard Suzy crying.

Aly felt her stomach sink, as if *she* were the one getting in trouble. That was the worst feeling, disappointing your parents—especially when it wasn't on purpose.

"Maybe Sophie was right," Brooke said quietly. "Maybe we should've tried harder to be friends with Suzy."

A few minutes later Suzy came into the kitchen with their records folder. She was still crying a little, and she wasn't even trying to hide it. "I was going to give your files back," she said. "And once everyone was here, I was going to call you. I just . . . It's just . . . everyone liked the idea of a pool party, and you wouldn't listen, so I . . . I did it myself."

"Thanks," Aly said, taking the folder. "It *was* a good idea, Suzy. But when you're working somewhere, you can't just do whatever you want and take whatever you want. And you definitely can't keep secrets from the people who are running the business."

"You kept the extra surprise for the soccer party a secret from me," Suzy said. "And you acted like I wasn't even a real part of your salon."

Yikes, that hurt. But Aly thought about what Suzy said. She wasn't entirely wrong.

"You're right," Aly told her. "I'm sorry about that.

But you have to learn how to be on a team if you want people to trust you. Anyway, let's get through this party, and then it won't even matter, because after today your internship is over."

"I know that, Aly," Suzy said. And for a second, Aly thought Suzy sounded sorry that her time at the Sparkle Spa was over.

After the last Angels player got out of the pool, Brooke announced: "The exciting parts of the party are officially starting! We have pizza, Unicorn Treat cookies, polka-dot manicures and pedicures, bracelet-making supplies, and . . . a surprise photo booth!"

"Photos? Cool! Are you going to e-mail them to us later?" Mia asked.

Brooke shook her head. "It's magic! You get to see them right after they're taken."

"Awesome!" Mia said. "I want to go first."

* * * * *

The photo booth was the most popular part of the party, and the soccer girls took a ton of pictures wearing Celegrape Good Times on their fingernails with Not Number Blue polka dots. They liked that color combination the best. And they liked the Unicorn Treat cookies, too.

"I can't believe we can eat glitter," Giovanna, who played defense, said as she took a second cookie.

"Isn't that the best?" Brooke agreed as she took a second cookie herself.

Before the team left, Jenica took Aly aside. "Great party, Aly. It totally made us feel like champions."

Aly smiled. And she even smiled a little at Suzy. Because Suzy Davis did have good ideas. Aly didn't think she'd ever get to hear any more of them, and she was kind of okay with that, but still, she had to give Suzy the credit she deserved.

＊　＊　＊　＊　＊

That night, it felt *so* good to be in bed. Brooke told Aly she didn't even have to brush and braid her hair. Both girls just wanted to go to sleep.

But then Mom and Sparkly came in. Sparkly jumped up on Brooke's bed, and Mom sat on the end of Aly's.

Ever since the girls had arrived home, Aly had been thinking about Suzy and her mom. She figured all Suzy had been trying to do was make her mom proud of her. But she just didn't do it in quite the right way.

"Mom," Aly began, "if we didn't run the Sparkle Spa anymore, would you still love us?"

"What kind of question is that?" Mom asked. "Of course I would."

"But . . . would you still be proud of us?"

"You two are sweet and kind and funny and smart,

and I'm proud to be your mom every day. I think it's great that you have your own business, but that's not why I'm proud of you. I'm proud of the people you are, not the things you do."

"We're proud of the people you are too, Mom," Brooke said. "Right, Aly?"

Aly laughed. And then she thought about their mom sticking up for them with Mrs. Washington. "I'm really glad you're our mom," she said.

"Me too," Brooke said.

And for the first time ever, Aly thought about how glad she was to be herself.

How to Give Yourself (or a Friend!) a Polka-Dot Pedicure

By Aly (and Brooke!)

* . * * . * * . * * . * * . * *

What you need:

Paper towels

Polish remover

Cotton balls

(or you can just use more paper towels)

Clear polish

One base color polish

(We recommend a darker polish for the base.)

One polka-dot color polish

(We recommend a lighter color for the polka dots. But if you pick a light base, then we recommend darker for the polka dots.

Basically, the polka dots should contrast with the base. That way you'll be able to see them better.)

A toothpick

(Actually, you might want a few toothpicks.)

What you do:

1. Put some paper towels on the floor—or wherever you're polishing—so you don't have to worry if it drips or spills. (Did you know that if you try to use polish remover on a couch, it sometimes gets rid of the polish you spilled, but it also gets rid of the color in the couch fabric? We didn't always know that, but now we do. . . .)

2. Take one cotton ball or a piece of paper towel and put some polish remover on it. If you have polish

on your toes already, use enough to get it off. If you don't, just rub the remover over your nails once to remove any dirt that might be on them. This makes the nail polish stick better. (Also, you don't want dirt to make lumps in your polish!)

3. Rip off two more paper towels. Twist the first one into a long tube and weave it back and forth between your toes to separate them a little bit. Then do the same thing with the second paper towel on your other foot. You might need to tuck the end of the paper towel under your pinkie toe if it pops up and gets in your way while you polish. (Once, I forgot this part and my pinkie polish rubbed off all over my ring toe.)

4. Open up your clear polish and apply a coat on each nail. Then close the clear bottle up tight. (You can do your toenails in any order, but

Aly usually starts with my big toes and works her way to my pinkies.)

5. Open the polish you're going to use as your base. Apply one coat on each toenail. Close the bottle up tight.

6. Repeat step five. Then let the polish dry for about five minutes. (If you know the "Ninety-Nine Bottles of Nail Polish on the Wall" song and sing it from ninety-nine down to sixty, you're probably dry enough.)

7. Open your polka-dot color and put the brush upside down somewhere on your paper towel where it won't make a mess. (We put it upside down so that any extra polish drips into the cap and not onto the paper towel.) Then dip a toothpick

into the polish and wipe off the extra. Use the polish on the toothpick to make a dot on your nail, and then dip and dot again and again until you have as many polka dots as you'd like. (You'll probably have a ton more on your big toenail than on your tiny pinkie toenail. Aly can usually get only one or two dots on my pinkie.) When you're done, close the bottle up tight.

8. Wait a few minutes (if you keep singing, I'd try to get down to thirty nail polishes on the wall), then open your clear polish. Apply a top coat of clear polish on all your toes. Close the bottle up tight. (You can go in the same order you did last time!)

9. Now your toes have to dry. You can fan them for a long time, or sit and make a bracelet or read a book or watch TV or talk to your friend (or sister!) until

you're all dry. Usually it takes about twenty min-utes, but it could take longer. (I'd start the Nail Polish on the Wall song from ninety-nine again, and then get all the way down to zero. You'll probably be dry by then, but you should touch your nail very carefully and see if it feels totally dry before you get up to do something else.)

And now, you should have a beautiful Polka-Dot Pedicure! Even after the polish is dry, you proba-bly shouldn't wear socks and sneaker-type shoes for a while. Bare feet or sandals are better so all your hard work doesn't get smooshed. (And then you can show everyone your polka dots!)

Happy polishing!

✳ ✳ ✳ ✳ ✳ ✳